IT
TAKES
COURAGE

by
Christine L. Schmitt

Illustrated by
Jami Moffett

Paulist Press
New York/Mahwah, NJ

Cover art by Jami Moffett

Cover design by Jim Brisson

Library of Congress Cataloging-in-Publication Data

Schmitt, Christine L., 1963-
    It takes courage / by Christine L. Schmitt.
        p.   cm.
    Summary: While at camp, Julia finds the courage to re-
veal to her friend Susannah that her father is beating her at
home.
    ISBN 0-8091-6624-0
    [1. Child abuse—Fiction. 2. Camps—Fiction.] I. Title.
PZ7.S3585It   1995
[Fic]—dc20   95-850
                                              CIP
                                              AC

Published by Paulist Press
997 Macarthur Boulevard
Mahwah, New Jersey 07430

Printed and bound in the
United States of America

*To peace,
love, and tolerance
in our world*

Savannah jumped out of bed the second her alarm clock went off. It was 8 a.m. and the bus would be arriving in an hour to take her to the first day of summer camp. She threw the sheets off her body and over her cat, Ariel, who was sleeping on the bed. Ariel leaped off the bed and scampered to the kitchen. Savannah crept into her mother's room.

"I'm up, Mom, I'm up! It sure is a lot easier to wake up for camp than for school!"

"Okay, honey. I'll get breakfast ready while you wash up."

Her mom then got out of bed, put on her robe and went downstairs to the kitchen. She no longer asked Savannah what she wanted for breakfast because her daughter had the same meal every day. "The usual," she would say. "The usual" consisted of peanut butter on toast and a big glass of apple juice. Savannah liked it so much that sometimes she brought a peanut butter and toast sandwich to school. By the time she ate it, it was cold. She loved it anyway.

As her mom was in the kitchen preparing breakfast, Savannah showered and got dressed. Since she was going to camp she could wear shorts, which her mom didn't let her wear to school. She remembered to put her bathing suit on under her clothes so she could go swimming. She decided to wear the shorts her mom had just cut from old jeans, and a white T-shirt. She thought of wearing her Keds but threw them back in the closet and put on her high tops instead.

Before Savannah went downstairs she experimented in front of the mirror. She tucked the shirt in, then took it out, then back in again. She pulled the shirt out one more time. She liked it better this way. She knew that her mom would tell her she looked like a "ragamuffin" and that she had to tuck the shirt back in. Her mom always said this.

Savannah ran downstairs and into the kitchen. Her toast and juice were already on the table. Her mom was at the counter pouring some milk into her coffee mug. Before she put the milk back in the refrigerator, she poured a little into a saucer for Ariel.

"I can't wait to go to camp today! Did you make my lunch? I hope I make a lot of friends! I can't wait to paint! Did you see the bus yet?"

Savannah was so excited and talked so much that she had not eaten any of her breakfast.

"Savannah-banana, you'd better start eating or you won't be ready when the bus gets here!"

There was no way Savannah was going to miss one day of camp, so she wolfed down her breakfast.

"What do you want for lunch, Savannah?"

"The usual, Mom."

"I knew it! I made it while I made your breakfast."

When Savannah finished her breakfast she put her dishes in the sink and placed her lunch in her knapsack. She bent down to pet Ariel who was finishing up the saucer of milk. Just as Savannah was about to pick her up, her mom

looked over and said, "Savannah, you look like a ragamuffin! Tuck in that shirt!"

"Mom!" Savannah whined.

"Savannah..." Her mom was then interrupted by the beeping of the bus horn.

"Mom, I gotta go!"

"Okay, dear. Have a good time! And tuck in that shirt!"

Savannah hugged her mom, gave her a kiss, then ran out the front door with her knapsack.

Savannah got on the bus, said hello to the driver, and walked to the back of the bus.

She thought she was the first kid on the bus but she was wrong. Crouched in one of the back seats was a small girl. She appeared to be sleeping but Savannah saw her eyes open slowly. The girl closed her eyes quickly when she realized she was being watched.

Savannah wasn't sure whether she should say hello or not. She remembered her mom telling her to treat other people the way she would want to be treated, so she said hello to the quiet girl. The girl remained silent and turned her body toward the side of the bus and away from Savannah.

Savannah, who had never been shy, sat down next to the girl. The girl tucked her chin even further into her chest. She pulled her feet up onto the dark green bus seat. Her arms were clutched around her knees.

Savannah ignored the obvious signs that this little girl did not want to be bothered. She turned toward her and said in a friendly tone, "Hi! My name is Savannah. What's yours?"

The little girl did not move or make a sound.

5

Savannah continued looking at the little girl in her faded blue jeans and gray long-sleeved sweatshirt. Her long blond hair was tied into a ponytail with a rubber band. She pulled the ponytail over her right shoulder in an attempt to hide her face. She looked like a turtle tucked tightly into its hard shell. Savannah remembered that a turtle will only poke its head out when it thinks no one is around. She decided to leave the girl alone for a little while.

Savannah turned her body toward the front of the bus. She stared straight ahead and wondered about this girl. Why would she wear jeans and a long-sleeved sweatshirt in the summer? It's not as though it's raining or anything, Savannah thought. Maybe she doesn't know we're gonna be running around all day. Maybe she has a change of clothes in her knapsack. She's gotta have a bathing suit.

Savannah looked around the bus. She had spent so much time wondering about this girl that she didn't see the bus was almost full. She called out to the kids she knew. Savannah was glad to see that everyone was as excited as she was about Camp Whisperwood. Well, everyone except for the girl next to her.

As she was thinking of what she could say to make this girl talk, the bus pulled into the camp. The driver stopped in front of a big oak tree. Nearly all of the kids grabbed their knapsacks, which contained their lunches, and raced out of the bus. Savannah stood up, but waited for this nameless girl to stand up and walk down the aisle of the bus. The girl put her knapsack over her right shoulder as she shuffled out of the bus.

"Julia," Savannah whispered. She saw the girl's name written on the knapsack. "Your name is Julia, isn't it?"

The girl paused when she heard Savannah call her name. "Wha...?" She realized what she had done and grabbed her knapsack tighter. She scurried off the bus like a frightened squirrel. Savannah was thrilled. She knew this was her name even if she wouldn't admit it.

"Your name is Julia, isn't it? I can see it on your knapsack."

Julia stopped in her tracks and turned to look at Savannah. "Don't you have anything better to do than to bother me? Can't you tell that I don't want to talk to you? I don't want to talk to anyone." Savannah was surprised at the tone of Julia's voice; she was only trying to be friendly.

Savannah's mom had told her one time that sometimes people get angry at someone because they are really angry at someone else. It made Savannah remember a time she was angry at one of her school friends and when she got home she yelled at her mom. Her mom didn't get mad at Savannah; she just asked Savannah why she was upset. Savannah told her mom what had happened on the way home from school. Just telling her mom about it made Savannah feel a lot better. She decided to try it with Julia.

Savannah returned Julia's look. "Why don't you want to talk to anyone? Aren't you excited about being at camp?"

"No," Julia's voice was much softer and quieter. "My parents only sent me here because they don't want me home. It's not as if I asked them to send me here."

"I love this camp! This is my third summer and I'm looking forward to coming back next summer too," Savannah explained enthusiastically. But it was a little too late. Julia had already started walking away. Well, at least she spoke to me, Savannah thought; that's a start.

Savannah decided to try one more time. "Julia, what group are you in? I'm in the Green group. Are you?"

Julia continued to walk in silence. She stared down at the ground most of the time, only glancing up once in a while. She only looked up so that she could find her group—the Green group.

Savannah followed Julia, thinking of what she could say to get her to talk. All of a sudden Julia stopped walking. Savannah bumped into her left arm. Julia pulled away quickly and winced. Savannah apologized.

"I'm sorry, I didn't mean to bump into you. I didn't know you were going to stop."

"Savannah! It's good to see you," Savannah's camp counselor from last year called to her. "So you're in my group again this summer. Who's your friend?"

"Her name is Julia. At least I think it is."

"Hi, Julia. My name is Tracey. Welcome to Camp Whisperwood."

Julia looked at Tracey blankly and then slowly lowered her head. Tracey said again, "Hi, Julia. I'm Tracey. I hope we can become friends."

Julia held onto her knapsack more tightly

and remained silent. Tracey looked over at Savannah and said, "Savannah, since you're an old pro, why don't you help Julia out the first few days?"

Savannah's face lit up. "Okay, Tracey, I can do that!"

Tracey looked at Julia and asked, "Julia, would you like that?"

Julia looked at Savannah and Savannah gave her a big smile. Julia returned a quick smile, but it was a smile at least. Julia looked up at Tracey and answered, "Yes, I guess so. That would be okay." Just as Tracey was leaving the two girls alone, Julia asked Savannah, "What's your name? Savannah?"

"Yep! That's it! Savannah, S-A-V-A-N-N-A-H!"

Tracey heard this exchange and turned around and smiled at Savannah. Then she turned her attention to the other campers.

"Okay, kids. Sit down. Let me introduce myself and tell you a bit about Camp Whisperwood."

All of the children, twenty of them, sat down around Tracey. Savannah sat next to Julia. Tracey told the children about all of the fun things they would be doing at camp this summer. When she began to explain about summer buddies, Savannah grabbed Julia's left arm and pulled it up in the air to let Tracey know they would be summer buddies. Julia yelled "Ow!" and yanked her arm down. Savannah let go of her hand. Julia turned away and looked at the ground. Tracey saw this and asked, "Is everything okay?"

"Yes," Julia answered softly.

"Are you sure?"

"Yes, I'm sure," Julia said a little more loudly.

Savannah apologized to Julia. She didn't think that she had pulled Julia's arm that hard. She hoped that this wouldn't make Julia hate her. She only wanted to be her friend.

The two girls sat in silence as Tracey finished talking about the camp. She told all of the kids to put their knapsacks in the big box next to her so they could get the day started. Their first activity was swimming.

As Tracey announced this, the kids buddied up and ran to the pool — all except Julia and Savannah. Julia was walking very slowly toward the box. She placed her knapsack inside and hesitated. Savannah went over to her and said, "C'mon, Julia. We're going swimming. You don't need a towel because the pool lady gives them to us."

Savannah reached for Julia's left arm but before she could grab it Julia turned away. I must really have hurt her arm, she thought.

"I'm sorry that I hurt you, Julia. I won't do it again."

Julia continued walking toward the pool. Tracey came up behind Savannah and said, "She's just shy, Savannah; she'll come around. Don't worry."

"Okay, Tracey, but I wish she would like me. I want to be her friend."

"Just give her time."

Tracey and Savannah followed Julia to the pool. The lifeguards were there, so all of the kids were already in the pool. No one was really swimming, just a lot of splashing and jumping around. Julia stopped at the pool gate. Tracey and Savannah caught up with her. "Julia, you can just leave your clothes in a little pile by the fence," Tracey suggested. "See where all of the other kids put their stuff?"

"I don't have a bathing suit on," Julia answered meekly.

"Your mom didn't remind you to put it on under your clothes? I never forget to do that!" Savannah was in disbelief.

"That's okay, Julia. We have some extra bathing suits in the pool house," Tracey offered. "Come with me and we'll find you one that fits."

"No, um, um, no...I...I don't know how to swim. That's what I meant to say."

"Well, we'll put you in the Tadpole swimming group. It'll just be a few days until you're out there with the rest of the group."

"Oh...I'll have to ask my mother. I don't think she wants me to swim. I'll ask her tonight when I go home."

"I can do better than that, Julia. I'll call her up at lunchtime and ask her myself."

Julia did not answer right away. Savannah thought Julia looked as though she had seen a ghost. She was staring straight ahead and her mouth was open. It looked as if she was trying to talk but no words came out. Suddenly Julia caught her breath and said, "You can't call her because she's at work." Julia looked a little bit calmer now.

"Don't worry, Julia. We have work numbers for everybody's parents, just in case there is an emergency."

"Okay, I guess. I hope she doesn't get mad if you call her at work."

"I won't be on the phone long enough for her to get mad. I'm sure she wants you to learn how to swim. Do you want to change into a bathing suit today or do you want to sit on the lounge chair next to me?"

"I'll sit in the chair."

"Wonderful. Savannah, why don't...?"

Tracey was going to tell her to go swimming, but it was too late. She was already playing games in the pool.

Savannah looked over at Julia and Tracey on the deck of the pool. Tracey was watching all of the kids but Julia was sleeping. Julia was sleeping! Savannah couldn't believe it! How could Julia sleep with so much fun going on around her? She began to wonder if she would ever understand Julia when the lifeguards blew the whistles. The kids all screamed "Boo! Boo!" No one wanted to get out of the pool. Tracey reminded them to obey the lifeguards. She told them that other groups had to use the pool.

As the kids dried off with their towels and got dressed, Savannah walked over to Julia. She brought her towel and clothes over to her lounge chair. Julia was still sleeping. Savannah shook her arm. Julia woke up immediately and looked at her. There were tears in her eyes. She was wiping them away with her sleeve but Savannah saw them.

"Julia, I didn't mean to hurt you. Please don't cry. I just want to be your friend."

"I'm not crying. Some of the water got in my eye. It must have happened when you guys were playing."

"Oh, I thought you were crying."

Savannah was almost positive that Julia was crying. She didn't know why Julia would be crying though, especially while at camp. This made Savannah remember how she felt her first day at camp two years ago. She was kind of homesick and almost cried a few times. But Tracey, who was her counselor then, too, was very friendly to her and encouraged her to play with the other kids. This had eventually made Savannah feel that she belonged in the group. Maybe that's all Julia needs too, she thought.

Julia waited while Savannah dried off and got dressed. All of the other kids were waiting for them outside of the pool gate. Savannah noticed that Tracey was watching them as they caught up with the group.

"Is everything okay, girls?"

"Yes, Tracey. Why?" Savannah asked.

"I was just wondering. You're being awfully quiet, Savannah."

"No, everything's okay, Tracey."

Everything's okay with me, she thought, but I don't know about Julia. She felt that if Julia wanted to tell Tracey that she was crying she could do it herself. She didn't want to be a tattletale. She also didn't think that would help to make Julia her friend.

"Julia, how about you?"

"I'm okay. There's nothing the matter with me."

She sure is good at lying, Savannah thought. I almost believe her myself.

Tracey turned to all of the kids and asked them

to sit on the grass. Julia sat down in the back of the group. Savannah sat near her because she wanted to figure out if she had been crying or not. While all of the kids were chattering and getting settled Savannah kept an eye on Julia. She had to do it just right because she didn't want Julia to know what she was up to. Savannah ignored all of the other kids around her. She made up her mind that she was going to figure this out.

Tracey turned to the group and said, "Okay, kids, quiet. I want to make something clear to you guys. If anyone has a problem while at camp, or if there is anything you want to talk about, I am here to listen." Savannah saw Julia look right at Tracey and not at the ground. Maybe, thought Savannah, she'll tell Tracey why she was crying. Tracey continued, "I am here to be your friend and I am also here to help all of you. If I can't give you the help that you need, then I promise I will keep looking until I find someone who can."

Tracey was looking at everyone while she spoke. When she was just about at the end of her speech, Savannah saw her look right into Julia's eyes. Julia returned Tracey's gaze briefly before she once again looked down at the ground. For a moment, there was silence.

Then Tracey clapped her hands. "Okay, group! Enough talking! Let's get moving! We're going to the softball field in ten minutes!" Laughing and talking excitedly, most of the kids stood up and began to run, walk and jump to the field with their buddies, bubbling over with enthusiasm for Tracey. "I like Tracey, don't you?" "Yeah, she's cool!" Savannah heard some of the kids say. Tracey

14

is nice, thought Savannah. All of the kids in my group think she's great.

Savannah walked over to Julia where she found Tracey sitting on the ground next to her. "I'm fine," Savannah overheard Julia saying. "I'm just not used to this camp yet. In fact, I may not come back tomorrow. I might not ever want to come back."

Tracey placed her hand on Julia's knee and said, "Julia, please promise me that you will try the camp for the rest of the week. If Friday comes and you still don't like it, then I'll talk to your parents and the camp director. Maybe you won't have to come back next Monday."

Julia answered quickly, "No, no, I'll be here tomorrow. It's okay. I'll get used to it."

"You're gonna love it, Julia. You'll see," Savannah told her. "We get to paint, play softball, ride the ponies and do a lot of other fun stuff. C'mon, Julia."

"Savannah, hold your horses. Let Julia make her own decision."

Savannah couldn't believe that Julia was thinking about not going to camp. Savannah loved Camp Whisperwood. She wished she could go to camp all year, instead of going to school. She even dreamed of someday being a camp counselor.

"Maybe I just have to get used to it. I'm not used to going to camp. I won't cause any more problems."

"Julia, do you want me to talk to your mom or dad tonight and let them know how you feel?" asked Tracey.

"No, I don't want them to get mad." Savannah thought Julia was acting the way she did at the pool. Why would her parents get mad? Savannah thought to herself. She seems to be afraid of them. This doesn't make any sense she thought. Kids aren't supposed to be afraid of their own mom and dad. I wonder what the problem could be.

"Okay, Julia," Tracey continued, "I won't say a word to your parents. Instead I'll do what I can to make sure that you enjoy camp so much that you'll want to come back next year." Tracey smiled at Julia and Julia smiled back weakly.

"Julia, I'll race you to the softball field," Savannah shouted, "On your mark, get set...GO! The two girls ran to the field with Tracey close behind.

The other team was already at the field. Some of the kids were on the field throwing, catching and hitting. Savannah looked around for the kids who were doing what she liked to do—sliding into the bases. She found a small group of kids sliding between the bleachers and home base. Savannah grabbed Julia's right arm and galloped like a wild horse to this group.

Julia yelled "Wait!" but Savannah had already taken off. There was no stopping her. When Savannah got to the patch of dirt she slid her feet and put her hands toward the ground. Julia was unprepared for this and was pulled down by Savannah. She fell to the ground on her back and Savannah landed on top of her.

"Wasn't that fun, Julia? I love sliding and getting all dirty!" Savannah began to brush herself off and as she stood, she turned to look at Julia. Julia

17

was sitting on the ground and rubbing her left arm. She wasn't actually crying, but Savannah thought she looked close to tears.

"Julia, are you okay?" Savannah reached down to Julia. "Here, I'll help you up." Savannah put her arm out to Julia; they held hands and she stood up. She wiped the dirt off her jeans.

Tracey caught up with the two girls as they were brushing the dirt off themselves. She had just gotten to the bleachers when Savannah and Julia slid onto the ground.

"Savannah, Julia, what's going on here?" She sounded a little bit mad.

"Remember last year, Tracey? Don't you remember how good I was at sliding? I wanted to show Julia how to do it. Wasn't it fun, Julia?" Julia did not answer.

"Julia, are you okay?" Tracey asked.

"Yeah, I'm okay. It was fun." Julia's face was expressionless.

"Well, you don't look as if you thought it was fun, but I'll take your word for it. I guess a little bit of dirt, or in this case a lot of dirt, never hurt anybody." Tracey started to brush some dirt off of Julia. "Turn around, Julia, and I'll get the dirt off of your back." Before Julia could move, Tracey had reached around her and was wiping the dirt off her sweatshirt. Julia moved away from Tracey as she did this.

"That's okay, Tracey. I'll do it myself."

"Julia, I'm almost done. Besides, you can't reach your arms all the way to your back."

Savannah watched Julia as Tracey cleaned her off. Julia's shoulders were hunched back and

19

her teeth were clenched. Savannah wondered if Julia had hurt her back when she fell.

"I think Julia hurt herself when she fell, Tracey."

Tracey looked at Julia and asked, "Julia, do you want to see the nurse? Did you hurt your back? Maybe she should examine you to be sure you're okay. I'll bring you over there while the rest of the group plays softball. How about it?"

"No. I don't want to see the nurse. I'll be okay. Can I sit on the bleachers for a while instead of playing?"

"Are you sure?"

"Yes."

"Okay, Julia, I'll let it go this time, because I think you'll enjoy watching the game. But if it looks to me as if you're still sore later, I'll have to insist on bringing you to the nurse."

"I know I'll be okay."

Julia sat down on top of the bleachers while Tracey and Savannah joined the two teams and the other counselor on the side of the field. The teams decided who would be first at bat and who would be in the field. After a few innings, Tracey motioned for Julia to join the game.

"No...no, not yet," said Julia. "I'm too hot and tired." She smiled convincingly, "Tomorrow I'll play, definitely."

Well, nothing could stop Savannah from playing softball. She loved that sport. Even when she didn't have to slide into a base she did. She especially liked to slide into home plate and pretend she had hit a home run. Yet today, even when Savannah was on the field, she couldn't stop thinking about

Julia. She wondered why Julia got hurt by every little thing, why she was wearing a sweatshirt in the hot summer and why she was so quiet all of the time. It seems almost as if she wants to be invisible, Savannah thought. Such a notion seemed unimaginable to Savannah because she liked nothing better than being the center of attention.

She looked over at Julia once in a while. She saw Tracey with her a few times. At least she's watching the game, Savannah thought, and not talking about leaving camp again.

The game finally ended and the Green group lost. Three players on the other team had hit home runs. Savannah was disappointed. She realized that instead of sliding she should really practice hitting. I'll ask Mom to pitch the ball to me every night after dinner so I can practice my hitting. Then we'll have a chance at winning, she decided. This gave Savannah an idea and she ran over to Julia.

"Julia, how about coming with me and my mom to the park on Saturday? My mom's a really good pitcher. We could practice hitting so that our team will be the champions this summer."

"I don't know, Savannah. I'll have to ask my father."

"My mom will talk to him. She'll convince him. She'll even pick you up at your house and bring you home. How could he say no to that?"

"I don't know, Savannah."

"C'mon, it'll be fun."

Julia looked at the ground, then at Savannah, and answered, "Okay, I'll ask him, but don't tell your mother to call. I don't want my father to get mad."

"I don't think he'll get mad, but whatever, make sure you ask him."

"Don't worry."

Savannah and Julia joined the other kids who were putting the softball equipment away. After the balls, bats, bases and mitts were locked up, the group walked over to the dogwood tree. Tracey asked each of the kids to sit with their buddy. She told them that she had planned a special activity for them.

"Does anyone know what a scavenger hunt is?"

There was a lot of mumbling among the kids and a lot of "no's."

"What's a scavenger hunt?" someone asked.

"Well, I'll explain what a scavenger hunt is. It starts out where I give each of the buddy teams a list of things that they have to find. Everybody has the same list, so no one will have it any easier or harder than anyone else. I'll show you the list in a little while. Now, when you get the list, you read it so you know what's on it. Then, when I say "Go!" all of the teams go off and try to find each item that's on the list. I'll give you a paper bag to put the stuff in when you find it. After you've found everything on the list, I want you to run back here and show me so I'll be sure that you found the right things. The first buddy team who finds everything on the list wins. Any questions?"

"How do we know what we're supposed to find?" someone asked.

"Well, remember I said I would give you a list? Here it is!"

Tracey handed each team of buddies a paper bag and an index card with six items on it. She handed a card to Julia. Savannah asked Julia to read it out loud.

"It says a dogwood leaf, a dried leaf, two bird feathers, a yellow dandelion, a white rock and a piece of a bird eggshell. This is gonna be fun!"

"I think so, too. I like this kind of stuff," Savannah said.

"Kids, I don't want you climbing trees for any of this. Everything can be found on the ground..."

"Not the bird eggshell," Savannah yelled out.

"Yes, even the bird eggshell. When the baby birds are born the shells fall to the ground. The only thing that won't be on the ground is the dogwood leaf, but the branches are low enough for all of you to reach. So, I do not want to see anybody climbing the trees."

After Tracey said that, there was a lot of moaning and groaning from the group. Tracey told the teams that they could not take anything out of anyone else's hands or bags. She said that would be like stealing. She reminded them that as soon as they got everything, they should run back to her as fast as possible.

"Ready?"

"Ready!" screamed the children.

"1, 2, 3, Go!" and the game began.

Before running off like the others Savannah pulled a leaf off of the dogwood tree. Julia held the bag out to her and she dropped it in quickly.

"Let's go, Julia! I remember seeing some dandelions on the softball field!"

Savannah galloped off, with Julia close behind holding the list and the bag. She crumpled the top of the bag so the leaf wouldn't fall out. Savannah was looking at the softball field, so she didn't notice the dried leaves on the ground that Julia saw.

Julia called out to her, "Savannah, do you think these leaves are dry enough?"

Savannah stopped running and glanced back at Julia. "Look dry enough to me. Throw them in the bag, Julia, and follow me."

Savannah continued toward the field while Julia looked for the driest leaf she could find. She wanted to make sure she didn't make any mistakes. She knew that Savannah wanted to win and she didn't want to be the reason they lost. She didn't want her buddy to get mad at her. With the leaves in the bag, held tightly in her hand, Julia caught up with Savannah by the pitcher's mound.

"What'd I tell you, Julia. Look at this. Which one should we pick?"

Savannah reached down and plucked a dandelion from the ground.

"Here's our dandy lion, Julia. Get it? Dandy lion?"

"Oh, that's funny, Savannah. I read a book once about Dandy the lion. Did you?"

"Yeah, that's where I got it from. Did you think I made it up? I'm not that smart. Okay, so far we have three things. What's next?"

"There are three more things, but four altogether. Two feathers, a white rock and an eggshell."

"Where are we gonna find an eggshell?" Savannah wondered.

"I think we should look under a tree where birds live. Maybe we'll find some feathers there too. Right?"

"Wow, you're a smarty, Julia. That's a good idea."

"You think so?"

"Yeah, of course."

"Really? Thanks. No on ever said that to me before." Julia smiled when she said this. Savannah was very excited to see Julia look happy. I think she likes me, Savannah thought.

"We should go to a tree with a lot of leaves. I think that's where birds live."

"Okay, let's go!"

The girls walked around looking up into the trees. A lot of the trees were skinny and didn't have many leaves.

"Do you hear that, Savannah?"

"What? What do you hear?"

"I think it's a bird. Come over here." Julia walked to the side of the building and looked up into the tree. "Listen." Savannah could hear a noise. It sounded like a bird chirping. "Does it sound like a bird to you, Savannah?"

"Yeah, I think so, Julia. Well, if a bird lives up there then there's got to be feathers around here. Let's look."

It didn't take long before Savannah and Julia each found a feather. Both of the feathers were brown with some white on them. There were about eight feathers in all.

"Julia, do you think we should take all of the feathers so that no one else can get any? Then we'll definitely win."

"I don't think that's fair, Savannah. Don't worry, we'll win. We're the best team anyway."

"Oh, you sound like my mother, but I guess you're right. We only have two more things to find anyway."

"Wait, Savannah, don't you think that if a bird lives here, that there may be eggshells around here too. Let's look around."

"Good idea, but be careful that you don't step on them and crush them."

The girls went off in opposite directions around the big tree. Savannah heard some other kids headed toward the building.

"Julia, we have to hurry up. Those guys are coming here. We have to find the eggshell before they do!"

"Don't worry, Savannah, I found it already. Here it is!"

Julia was holding a big piece of an eggshell in the palm of her hand. Savannah reached out to grab it.

"You have to be gentle with it, Savannah, or it will break." Julia slowly placed the eggshell in the bag. They were on their way to find a white rock now.

When they passed by the other kids, one of them said, "Did you find anything over here?"

"Maybe and maybe not," Savannah giggled.

"We're not telling." Savannah ran off but slowed down when Julia called after her.

"Savannah, slow down. Remember?" Savannah forgot that Julia didn't want the eggshell to break, so she stopped running. Savannah was too excited to walk slowly, so instead she walked as fast as she could. We have to win this, she thought. Only one more thing.

Julia was thinking the same thing: Maybe we'll win after all.

Julia caught up with Savannah. "I remember seeing white rocks somewhere, Savannah. Do you?"

Savannah thought for a moment and then said, "Follow me!" She walked quickly, but didn't run, toward the pool. At the bottom of the fence all around the pool were white rocks. Savannah picked up the whitest rock she could find.

"Open up the bag, Julia. I'll drop it in and we're done."

"Maybe you should hold the rock in your hand, Savannah. I think it will break the eggshell."

"You're right. Let's go!"

Savannah raced toward Tracey while Julia followed behind her a little more slowly. When Julia got to Tracey, Savannah was telling Tracey that they found everything on the list.

"Julia, why don't you take everything out of the bag and I'll check it out."

"Okay, Tracey."

First Julia took out the eggshell and placed it on the ground next to the white rock that Savannah had carried.

"You found the eggshell. That's fantastic! I

wasn't even sure anyone would find one. I'm surprised!"

Julia removed the two feathers, the two leaves and the dandelion from the bag. Tracey looked at all the items and congratulated the girls. "We have the winners!" she yelled out. "I want everyone to keep looking. Let's see who comes in second and third place."

Savannah and Julia played with the feathers until the second and third place teams were done. Tracey told everyone she was glad that no one had climbed any trees or taken things from anyone else. Then she said what they all wanted to hear, "Time for lunch!"

The box with all of the lunches in it was by the dogwood tree. Tracey told everyone to sit down while she passed out the lunches. Savannah and Julia sat next to each other and opened their lunches. Savannah flattened her brown bag on the ground and placed her sandwich, cookies and juice on top of it. She was removing the sandwich from the plastic bag when she saw what Julia was eating. "I can't believe it!" she gasped. "You're eating peanut butter on toast!"

Julia lowered the sandwich from her mouth and put it on her bag. She began to cover it with a napkin when Savannah screeched, "That's what I have! That's my favorite! I never met anyone else who liked it! I mean, I know other kids who like peanut butter on hot toast, but not cold!" Savannah held her sandwich up to Julia's face so she could see for herself. Julia leaned back as Savannah stuck the sandwich in her face. She started laughing and so

29

did Savannah. "We're meant to be friends after all, Julia."

"I guess so, Savannah."

Both girls started eating their sandwiches. They had to stop laughing so they could chew the food. As Julia reached for her juice, she said, "What kind of juice do you have?"

"What kind do you have?"

"I asked you first. What kind do you have?"

"Apple juice. How about you?"

"Me too. Apple juice! We could be sisters!"

The two new friends finished their lunches between giggles. Savannah was glad that Julia was laughing now, instead of crying. Maybe she really did just have water in her eyes, Savannah thought, but she sure looked as though she was crying.

After what seemed like a very short time, Tracey called out loudly, "Time for arts and crafts! Throw your garbage out and then line up next to me at the oak tree!"

"You're gonna love arts and crafts, Julia. Painting is so much fun and you're allowed to get messy! My mom always makes me bring an extra T-shirt in case the one I'm wearing gets dirty."

"I didn't bring another shirt."

"Well, you can borrow mine if yours gets dirty. Don't worry."

After cleaning the lunch area, the group followed the narrow dirt path to the arts and crafts center. Inside, Savannah saw that the paints were set up. They were going to paint today. The arts and crafts counselor showed the kids how to clean the brushes and how to avoid dripping the paint on the floor. Once everyone seemed to understand they started painting.

Savannah decided to paint a picture of her cat, Ariel, near some flowers. She was being careful not to make a mess this time. She wanted to see if she could finish it without getting any paint on her shirt.

She looked over to see what Julia was painting. It looked as though she was painting a castle. Savannah was amazed at what a good job she was doing. Julia didn't tell her she was an expert! Savannah turned her attention back to her own painting. She was mixing the blue and white paints to get the perfect color for Ariel's eyes. If she finished the painting today she could bring it home and her mom would hang it on the refrigerator door.

"Oh no!" She heard Julia mutter. "Oh no!"

"What's the matter, Julia?"

"My sleeve went into the paint!"

"That's okay. Just roll up your sleeve and finish your picture. It looks great! You can change into my other shirt when you're done."

"No, I can't do that. What if I ruin it?" Julia answered nervously.

"You won't ruin it."

"No, I'll just wear this."

"You sure?"

"Yeah, I'm sure."

"Everything okay, Julia?" Tracey asked as she surveyed all the children.

"Oh, it's nothing, nothing. I just got some paint on my sweatshirt. It's okay."

"You can't wear that for the rest of the day. Did you bring another shirt?"

"No, she didn't," Savannah jumped in. "But she can wear mine. My mother won't mind."

"No, I don't want to! I'll just wear the sweatshirt." She started crying. "Just leave me alone. Leave me alone!"

Julia sat down on the floor and leaned against the wall. All of the other kids had stopped painting and were watching Tracey, Savannah and Julia. Savannah followed Julia over to the wall. She bent down on her knees and put her arm around her. She could feel Julia's shoulders trembling under her touch. She seems so scared, Savannah thought. What happened? Is she upset over some silly paint? Savannah was very confused. She saw Tracey's feet and looked up to see Tracey right next to them. "Honey, please tell me what is really wrong. I'm here to help you. I promise," said Tracey softly.

Tracey's loving tone reminded Savannah of how her mom sounded when she was comforting her. Apparently this was not helping Julia, who had begun to cry. "Julia, I want to be your friend. I want to help you. How about if you and Savannah go and talk in the back room. You can talk privately there."

Julia sniffled and reached out to grasp Tracey's extended hand. Julia had been crying so much that her sleeves were wet with paint and tears. With Tracey's help she stood up. Then she grabbed hold of Savannah's hand and held onto her tightly. Together they walked to the back room and sat down.

"I'm sorry, Savannah, I'm sorry," said Julia

wiping her face. "You'll never want to be my friend now. No one will like me."

"Julia, that's not true. I just wish you would tell me what's the matter."

Julia was very quiet.

"I can only tell you if you promise not to tell anyone."

"Okay, I won't."

"Even if someone is doing something bad, something really bad?"

"Sure. Whatever you say."

"But I don't think anyone can help me," Julia responded.

"Well, if we tell a grown-up maybe they could help you. Did you tell your mom? What did your mom say?"

"She won't do anything."

"Maybe if you tell me, I can find someone who can help."

"Do you think so?" she asked sadly, "Do you really think you can help me?"

"I'll do the best I can. But I wish you would tell me."

Julia looked up at Savannah. Her eyes were red and swollen from crying. She glanced down at the floor, took a deep breath, and then another one. She held her hands together in her lap and stared straight at Savannah.

"This is really hard for me to say, so I think I should show you." She took another deep breath. "Do you still have that T-shirt?"

Savannah handed her the shirt. As Julia started to remove her sweatshirt Savannah turned away. She thought Julia would want some privacy.

34

"Okay. You can look now."

Julia was wearing Savannah's T-shirt. Her sweatshirt was crumpled in a pile on the floor. Savannah turned toward Julia and looked in her eyes. Her eyes were moist but not crying. It looked as if she was holding back tears. Julia looked down at the floor, then back up at Savannah. She lifted the sleeve of her shirt up.

Savannah couldn't believe what she saw. Julia's arm had purple and blue marks on it. They look worse than the bruises I get on my legs when I fall down while playing, thought Savannah. "What happened, Julia? Did you fall out of a tree?" she asked. "I didn't know you hurt yourself like that. When I bumped into you and pulled your arm up it must have really hurt. I'm so sorry," said Savannah.

"I know that."

"How did it happen?"

Julia let the shirt sleeve fall down. She rested her elbows on her knees and lowered her head into her hands. Savannah could hear her sniffling.

"My father...my father," Julia was talking very slowly and so low that Savannah almost didn't hear her.

"Your father what?"

"My father beat me." Julia sat up and looked at Savannah. "My father beat me."

"Your father beat you? What do you mean, he beat you?"

"I mean he beat me. He beats me a lot. That's how I got the bruises on my arm. He beat me. I was afraid to tell you because he said if I told anyone he would beat me harder."

"What does your mother say?"

"Nothing. She says nothing. She just watches him do it." She started crying. "I don't want to go home. I can't take it anymore. It just hurts so much."

"I think we should tell Tracey. She'll know what to do."

Julia continued sobbing.

"No, she can't help. Don't tell."

"She said she wanted to help, remember?"

"Do you really think she can help me?"

"Let's tell her," said Savannah. "She'll know what to do."

Savannah called Tracey into the back room. She walked in and knelt on the ground between the two girls.

"I think you should show her first," Savannah told Julia.

Julia pulled the sleeve up again. Tracey looked at the bruises silently. Why doesn't she look surprised? Savannah thought. Maybe she knew about this.

"I'm sorry, Julia. I'm sorry this happened to you, but I need to ask you if you have any other marks on your body."

Julia turned her back to Tracey and started to lift up her shirt.

"Do you want me to look, Julia? Is it okay?"

"Yes," she whispered.

Tracey gently lifted up Julia's shirt. Savannah stood next to her and looked at her friend's back. It was awful. There were a lot of terrible-looking marks on her back. Some were purple and blue, some were green and yellow and some were brownish. Savannah was shocked. She was glad

37

that Tracey was here because she seemed calm and in control. Tracey lowered Julia's shirt tenderly.

"Turn around, Julia," she said. "We need to talk. Julia, I want to help you. I know this is going to be hard, but I want you to tell me exactly what happened. Do you think you can do that?"

"I'll try." Julia was still fighting back her tears. She looked at Savannah and held her hand. The two girls exchanged nervous looks and then Julia looked at Tracey. She squeezed Savannah's hand tightly, then relaxed it. She took a deep breath and started speaking.

"My father beats me when he gets mad. Sometimes I do something wrong and sometimes I don't. I'm just sitting there watching TV and he starts yelling at me. He takes off his belt, or he tells me to get a belt from the closet. He says, 'Take off your shirt! You're gonna get a beating." Then he hits me with the belt. I used to cry and ask him to stop, but that didn't work, so I just take it. My mother doesn't even try to help. In the beginning, when I was five, she would ask him to stop. She'd say, 'Please, honey, she's only a baby,'" but he would ignore her. So she doesn't do anything about it anymore. She just sits in the kitchen and turns the radio up loud. When he's done he tells me to go to my room because he doesn't want to see my face. So I go to my room...I don't know...sometimes...I don't know. I usually get my paper and crayons and draw another place — a better place. Then I think about leaving my house and going there. I draw a castle and pretend I'm a princess. I just imagine

38

that one day, when I am grown up, I can go away and live in a castle like that."

Savannah was speechless. First Julia wouldn't talk and now she says all this. Savannah looked up at Tracey. She seems so sad, thought Savannah. Tracey reached over to hold Julia's hands. Savannah let go of her hand and watched as Tracey held them in her own.

"Julia, you're a very brave girl to tell us what happened to you. It took a lot of courage. It makes me very sad that this has been going on for four years, but I'm glad that you have decided to talk to me. Now we can work together and see what we can do to change your situation."

The three of them walked out of the back room. Tracey spoke privately with the arts and crafts counselor. Savannah rejoined the group of campers and Tracey and Julia went to talk to the director of the camp. The counselor told the group that she would be with them for the rest of the day. Savannah felt a little bit left out, but she knew that this was something that needed a grown-up. She was glad that Tracey was going to help Julia.

On the way home from camp Savannah thought a lot about what had happened. She thought about when she got on the bus in the morning and first met Julia. Julia was so quiet then. She wouldn't talk to me at all, Savannah remembered; she wouldn't even look at me. She now realized that the way Julia was acting actually made sense. If she couldn't trust her own father to be nice to her, then I guess I couldn't expect her to trust me. She probably figured that if someone who loves

her hurts her a lot, then she can't count on some-one she doesn't even know to be nice to her.

I guess it's the same thing with her mother too. If someone was treating me badly, I know, definitely, that my mom would put a stop to it immediately. But Julia's mom didn't do that. It must be scary to live in a house like that, where a kid needs one parent in order to be protected from the other parent. I thought that every kid lived in a home that was safe. I guess I should be thankful that my mom loves me so much.

Savannah was thinking about how she was go-ing to tell her mom all of this as the bus pulled up in front of her house. Her mom was at the end of the driveway waiting for her. Since Julia wasn't on the bus, Savannah was the last kid to be dropped off. She said goodbye to the bus driver and walked toward her mom. As the bus was pulling away she and her mom waved to the driver.

Savannah and her mom walked toward each other and hugged. Her mom was about to let go when Savannah gave her one more tight hug.

"Wow! You sure missed me, didn't you?" her mom said in surprise. "Will I get this greeting every day? I sure like it."

Savannah loosened up her hug, but didn't let go of her mom's waist. She looked up at her mom and said, "You are not going to believe what hap-pened at camp today! I have to sit down to tell you. It's such a long story."

Placing her hands on her daughter's shoul-ders, her mom responded, "Well, let's get going. I already took the chocolate chip ice cream out of the freezer so it would be a little soft when you

arrived home. I know how much you like to scoop out your own ice cream, young lady." Her mom gave Savannah a kiss on her forehead.

Savannah removed her hands from around her mom's waist and they walked hand in hand to the front porch, up the stairs, through the house and into the kitchen. Savannah took two bowls from the cupboard while her mom took the ice cream off the windowsill. The scooper and two spoons were already on the kitchen table. Savannah's mom put the box of ice cream in front of Savannah so she could scoop out the amount she wanted. After she took out her portion Savannah slid the box over to her mom. Savannah picked up her spoon and was just about to scoop out some ice cream that had a lot of chips in it. But she put the spoon down.

"I have to tell you what went on today before I eat. I thought about it the whole way home."

Her mom was returning the ice cream to the freezer. "Okay, sweetie, tell me what happened."

Savannah started out from the very beginning — about the bus ride to camp that morning — to the last thing she knew — that Tracey was bringing Julia to speak with the director of the camp. "Now I'm scared though, because Julia wasn't on the bus on the way home. What if Tracey told Julia's father what she said? He said he would hurt her even worse and it would be all my fault because I made her say it. She didn't even want to tell us. Did I do something wrong? I only wanted to be her friend."

Her mom placed her hand on her shoulder and said, "Honey, you did everything just right.

You behaved the way a friend is supposed to behave. Julia wanted to tell someone because she wanted her father to stop hitting her with the belt. She just didn't know how to tell anyone. She didn't know if she could trust you at first. It takes a lot of strength for children to tell someone if a parent, or any adult, is hurting them."

"That's almost the same thing that Tracey said, except that she said, 'It takes a lot of courage.'"

"Well, Tracey is a very smart young woman because she is exactly right. Julia would not have gotten any help if she didn't tell someone what was happening to her at home. She just needed the right person around to tell — and that person was you. I'm very proud of you, Savannah."

"Really?"

"I sure am. I have an idea I think you'll appreciate. Would you like me to call Tracey and find out what happened?"

"Can you do that?"

"I'm sure Tracey told the director about how you helped out Julia. They're probably expecting you to call."

Savannah's mom called the camp. She was on the phone for a long time. Savannah was getting impatient. Finally her mom said goodbye and hung up the phone.

"Well, what happened?"

"I spoke with Tracey. She said that after Julia spoke with the camp director they decided to place a telephone call with Child Protective Services."

"What's that?"

"Child Protective Services is a place where

people work to help children who get hurt like Julia."

"You mean there are a lot of kids like Julia?"

"Yes there are, Savannah. Unfortunately there are many children who do not feel safe in their own homes. These children are often afraid to tell anyone about what is happening to them in their homes. That's why I am so proud of you. Julia would not have told you about her father if she didn't trust you."

"I didn't know it was such a big deal. I'm glad I was able to help her. When Tracey and Julia left the arts and crafts center some of the kids came over to me and asked me what Julia said to me. Now I'm glad I didn't tell them. I told them that they could ask Tracey."

"That was the correct thing to say, Savannah. Julia trusted you with that information and I'm sure that she would appreciate you keeping that information to yourself."

"But I told them to ask Tracey," Savannah said worriedly.

"Don't worry. Tracey will tell them as much as she feels they need to know. She will respect Julia's privacy."

"Oh, good. I was a little nervous. So...is Julia going to go home tonight or is she going to sleep at the camp?"

"Let's back up a bit. After Tracey called Child Protective Services someone from there called Julia's parents."

"What! They told her parents! This doesn't sound too good, mom."

"Slow down, Savannah. Julia has an aunt and

an uncle who live close by. She is going to live with them for a while. In the meantime, people from Child Protective Services will talk to Julia's parents to get more information, and have some kind of an investigation."

"Is she going to live with her aunt and uncle forever?"

"Maybe and maybe not," her mom answered. "If Julia's parents want her to live with them again, then they will have to get something called counseling. This means that her mother and father will go to a counseling center where they will talk with another person about their problems. They will also learn how to work out their problems. This person will try to teach her parents that they can't hit Julia anymore, or allow her to be hit anymore. Her mother needs to learn that she has to protect her child. Her father will learn that he should not hit Julia because he is mad. When she gets in trouble he should just punish her by not letting her watch TV or not letting her go out to play. He should never, ever hit her with a belt."

"So her parents have to do all this to get Julia back home?"

"Yes, and Julia will go to counseling too. Her counselor will help her to understand that she did not deserve to be hit. Right now she thinks she was bad and that her father was right to hit her. That is not true. The counselor will help Julia to become happy again."

"Can I still see Julia?" Savannah asked hopefully.

"Of course, sweetie. Tracey gave me her aunt's

phone number. Julia wants you to call her. Here it is!"

Savannah snatched the paper out of her mom's hand. She ran to the phone and dialed Julia's new phone number. Savannah was looking forward to her new friendship with Julia.